BILLY
GHAST

The blurred figure Billy and Keith saw rising from the grave with a halo of light behind it looked terrifying. Not only was it covered in soil, but the left side of its face was a blank, greyish-white – bare bone!

"Garf!" it yelled. "Wargh, wumpf – waaarf!"

"Arrrgh!" shrieked the two boys.

"Woooaah!" yelled the dreadful figure, and it lifted up a hand and began to peel back its ghastly grey-white skull.

"It's – it's – a g-g-ghost!" screamed Keith.

"Oi!" yelled the awful spectre. "Come back!" And it began to stride across the graveyard towards them.

Also by Mick Gowar

BILLY AND THE MAN-EATING PLANT

BILLY AND THE GHASTLY GHOST

Mick Gowar

Illustrated by Celia Canning

RED FOX

A Red Fox Book
Published by Random House Children's Books
20 Vauxhall Bridge Road, London SW1V 2SA

A division of Random House UK Ltd

London Melbourne Sydney Auckland
Johannesburg and agencies throughout the world

First published by Macmillan Children's Books 1990

Red Fox edition 1992

Printed and bound in Great Britain by
Cox & Wyman Ltd, Reading, Berkshire

ISBN 0 09 981490 0

One

It was a hot Monday afternoon in the last week of June. Brilliant sunshine flooded through the tall Victorian windows of Holebridge School. In the school kitchens the extra heat made the dinner-ladies fuss and snap at each other as they cleared away and washed up in their steamy sauna. Along the corridors and into the classrooms a sleepy warmth drifted like an invisible mist. In the "Resources Area" Mrs Gurdon nodded off as her class watched *Adventures in Algebra* with drooping eyelids. In the Infant classroom the smallest children were already fast asleep.

Only Class Four, Mr Parker's third and fourth year Juniors, didn't seem to notice the heat. They were listening, entranced, as Mr Parker read to them from the *Tales of King Arthur's Knights*. He had been reading a chapter or two each day for the past two weeks, and they'd now come to the last chapter. The final battle was over and the Fellowship of the Round Table had been destroyed. Mordred and most of the knights were dead and King Arthur himself lay mortally wounded. As Mr Parker read, the children could feel the icy breath of winter.

1

They could see the dark clouds gathering over the stricken land. Twice the king had told Sir Bedivere to throw Excalibur into the lake, and twice Sir Bedivere had returned unable to do as his king had commanded. Night was falling fast. Soon the darkness would come, a darkness that would last for two hundred years. Mr Parker read on:

Across the still, deep waters of the lake the grey mist was getting thicker.

Sir Bedivere left the dying king and, for the third time, walked slowly down to the lakeside carrying the great sword Excalibur. This time, he knew, he must do the King's bidding.

Sir Bedivere raised the great sword as if in a final salute, and then threw it with all his strength towards the centre of the lake, as the King had commanded.

But the sword did not fall into the water. A hand and an arm clothed in a long white sleeve rose from the centre of the lake. The hand caught Excalibur by the hilt. Three times the great sword was waved aloft. Then sword, hand and arm slowly disappeared – down, down into the dark waters.

Sir Bedivere watched until the ripples had died away to nothing and the waters of the lake were still again. Then he walked back through the reeds and the sedge to where the King lay.

"The time has come," whispered King Arthur. "Good Sir Bedivere, carry me to the water's edge."

As Sir Bedivere carried the King down to the lakeside he saw a black barge moving silently across the dark water. Seated in the barge were three queens, dressed in black, their faces hidden behind long black veils. As the barge drew closer to the shore Sir Bedivere could hear that they were weeping.

"I must go with them," whispered King Arthur. "Lift me into the barge, Sir Bedivere, for I must sail to Avalon. Only there can my wounds heal . . . and if I do not return, pray for my soul."

Sir Bedivere lifted King Arthur into the barge. One of the queens laid the King's head in her lap. Then, as silently as it had arrived, the black barge sailed out towards the centre of the lake and disappeared into the mists.

Mr Parker closed the book. He looked around the room. The children were silent, scarcely daring to breathe. Then hands shot up and the silence was broken by anxious, eager voices:

3

"What happened next?"

"Please, Mr Parker, did King Arthur get better?"

"Did he die, Mr Parker? *Please* tell us, did he die . . . ?"

Mr Parker raised his hands for quiet.

"There are many different versions of the stories I've been telling you," he explained. "In one version Sir Bedivere discovers King Arthur's tomb some days later. The tomb is being guarded by a hermit – a holy man – who turns out to be the old Archbishop of Canterbury. The two men spend the rest of their lives keeping watch over the grave and praying. And there are other versions of the story which say that King Arthur and the Knights of the Round Table aren't dead at all but sleeping in a cave. And if ever England is invaded, or in great danger of some sort, they will all wake up and come to our rescue.

"Some people have actually claimed to have seen King Arthur's grave. It's said that the gravestone had a very peculiar inscription:

hic iacet Arthurus
rex quondam rexque futurus

"That's Latin, and it means, 'Here lies Arthur, king once and king to be,' or, 'The once and future king.'"

"So that's like saying that he *might* come back, isn't it?" asked Matthew Evans.

Mr Parker paused, and smiled at the children. "Yes, but don't forget everybody, it is only a story. Maybe there was a King Arthur, long, long ago. But he wouldn't have been anything like the King Arthur of the stories. He was probably the chief of a British tribe who fought the Anglo-Saxons, just after the Romans left. All the stories about King Arthur and the Knights of the Round Table were told, and added to, and retold many times before they were ever written down. No one knows how many of the stories are based on fact and how many were simply made up. But in the end, I don't suppose it really matters. After all, they are wonderful stories and that's what counts."

Mr Parker was interrupted by the bell ringing for the start of afternoon playtime.

"Right, that's enough for now. Off you go."

The children rushed out of the classroom. King Arthur and his Knights of the Round Table still had plenty of battles to fight in the playground that they hadn't managed to finish at lunchtime.

King Arthur and his toughest knight, Sir Lancelot, clattered over the drawbridge and out of the main school building. They wheeled

5

to the right, away from the main gates of the castle, and galloped across the playground towards the school kitchens. It was a school rule that children mustn't fight with sticks, so the two knights had hidden Excalibur and Sir Lancelot's sword behind the dustbins when the bell had rung for the end of dinner.

But ten metres from the hiding place they had to rein in their horses. One of the dinner-ladies was emptying a bucket of slops into a dustbin. The two mighty warhorses, Champion and Silver, pawed the ground impatiently. They could sense that, at that very moment, the dreadful Questing Beast was rampaging across the school field. It was heading for its lair beneath the long-jump pit, devouring everything and everyone in its way. Only King Arthur and Sir Lancelot could stop it.

Eventually the dinner-lady banged the lid back on to the dustbin and stomped back to the kitchens, slamming the door behind her. King Arthur and Sir Lancelot dismounted and scuttled across the playground in a crouching commando run.

Sir Lancelot kept watch while King Arthur drew the magical sword Excalibur out from behind the dustbin with a flourish. It was spattered with custard and gravy. The dinner-lady had missed the bin. Undaunted, King Arthur

wiped Excalibur clean with his shirt-tail. Then
the boys changed places and Sir Lancelot rooted
around behind the dustbin. He wasn't so lucky.

"Oh, no! Look at this." Keith Hall held up
his stick. Ten centimetres from the end there
was a jagged split. As he held it up the end
fell off and hung by a thin thread of bark.

"Someone's bust my sword. I'll have to get
another one."

He pulled off the dangling tip. He held up
the shortened sword and looked at it critically.

"I suppose it *might* do as a dagger." Keith
stabbed at the air to try it out. "But you
couldn't kill a Questing Beast with a dagger.
You'd never get close enough – it'd bite your
head off!"

But the King had spotted a new danger, a
danger far worse than a dragon or a Questing
Beast.

"Quick, Keith!" he yelled. "Christine Robinson
and those soppy girls are in our sand-pit!" And
the two boys sprinted across the field. They'd
forgotten all about their swords; they'd even
forgotten to mount their horses.

King Arthur and Sir Lancelot arrived red-
faced and gasping, but they were too late.
Christine Robinson and her best friend for today,
Deirdre, were already settled on the edge of
the long-jump pit. They were making daisy

7

chains and giggling about something – or some-one. Neelam Patel was sitting alone on the grass, a few metres away. She'd been Christine's best friend yesterday. Neelam was also plaiting daisies, but with a fierce concentration. Her eyes looked red and puffy. It was hard to tell whether she was part of the game the other two girls were playing or whether she just *happened* to be doing the same thing, at the same time, in the same part of the field.

"That's *our* place," protested King Arthur, still breathless from running. "We bags'd it at dinner. It's a dragon pit – you can't play here!"

Christine stood up and faced the two boys. With a queenly gesture, she smoothed down the nylon scarf which was pinned to her hair-band.

"My ladies-in-waiting and I got here first," Christine announced, and she made a regal sweep with her arm. The royal wave included both Deirdre and Neelam. Neelam shuffled closer to the sand-pit, her face glowing with relief and gratitude.

"So hard luck!" Christine continued. "We're here now, so you can just push off! Go and play your stupid dragon games somewhere else – *Billy Simpkins!*"

Two

It was four o'clock. Mr Fairbrother, the headmaster of Holebridge School, was in his study trying to sort out last week's dinner-money figures. The forms had been sent to the Council Offices – with all the money – last Friday. They'd come back today.

Mr Fairbrother stared in amazement at the sheet of paper in front of him. Someone at the Council Offices – a former teacher? Mr Fairbrother wondered – had marked it. Some of the numbers had been underlined in black; other numbers had been circled in green biro. The grand total was underlined three times in red, and, beside it, the "someone" had scrawled two question marks and three exclamation marks.

Mr Fairbrother could see why. The total was £22,690.16. It was engraved into a blob of Tipp-ex a quarter of an inch thick.

Mrs Wentworth, the school secretary, had done it again! Every week the dinner-money forms went out, and every week they came back again. Sometimes the total was over, sometimes it was under, and once – three years ago last

10

March – it was correct. But never, in five years of correcting Mrs Wentworth's sums, had Mr Fairbrother known her to get the total so spectacularly wrong.

He looked at the total again: £22,690.16. An idea slowly began to form in Mr Fairbrother's brain. He opened the top drawer of his desk and took out his diary.

"Let me see, last Friday's date was . . . " He scribbled down the numbers and did a subtraction sum in the margin of the forms.

"Hmmmm . . . " Mr Fairbrother frowned. It wasn't what he'd been hoping for. Last Friday's date accounted for £21,690 of the total, but the answer still wasn't right. He checked through the figures again, and tapped each number carefully into his calculator.

But for once he couldn't blame Mrs Wentworth. This time it was all *his* fault. It had been his idea that Mrs Wentworth should use Class Three's computer to add up the dinner-money – in fact, he'd insisted.

"All you have to do, Mrs Wentworth," he'd said, "is to type the figures in. The computer does all the adding up. The children will help you if you have any problems, but I'm sure you won't."

Mrs Wentworth hadn't looked very certain about that.

11

He'd done his best to reassure her. "Computers can't make mistakes. As long as you type in all the numbers on the list you can't go wrong. Whatever total the computer comes up with *must* be the right answer."

Mr Fairbrother pressed the "Total" button on his calculator. The new total flickered up at him, green and venomous: £10,674.16. It was no good; he was getting as bad as Mrs Wentworth!

With a sigh, Mr Fairbrother scooped up all the papers and the calculator and bundled them into his brief-case. He'd have to work on it tonight at home. Wearily, he put on his jacket, picked up his brief-case, and left the room.

Mr Fairbrother came out of the school entrance and began to walk across the playground towards his car. But as he came within sight of the school field Mr Fairbrother noticed something very strange going on in the long-jump pit. Two children appeared to be digging frantically in the sand with sticks. As Mr Fairbrother watched, one of them let out a great cry – "Aaaarrrrgh!" – and flung himself full-length into the pit, kicking and struggling.

"Good heavens!" thought Mr Fairbrother. "He's having a *fit*!" And he dropped his brief-case and began running across the field.

Billy and Keith saw Mr Fairbrother rushing towards them. Keith hurriedly scrambled out of the sand-pit. By the time Mr Fairbrother arrived, he was brushing the sand off his T-shirt and trousers.

"What on earth," spluttered Mr Fairbrother, "do you two boys think you're doing?"

Billy and Keith stared at the ground, thoroughly embarrassed.

"Well?"

"Dunno, sir," mumbled Billy.

"I can't hear you – speak up, Billy."

"I dunno, sir – just messing about."

Mr Fairbrother sighed and looked up at the sky. Typical! he thought. "Well, you can just go and 'mess about' somewhere else. It's after four, and you both know the school rules: no games after school unless there's a teacher with you. And *how* many times do I have to tell you? No playing with sticks! It's much too dangerous."

"Sorry, sir," mumbled Billy, again.

"Yeah, sorry, Mr Fairbrother," added Keith.

"Go on, off you go. Your parents will be wondering what's happened to you."

Mr Fairbrother watched the two boys trudge across the playground towards the school gates. He sighed and shook his head. He still hadn't got the faintest idea what they were up to and he didn't suppose he ever would.

* * *

Billy and Keith ambled slowly up the hill towards the church, dragging their swords behind them.

"Do you think . . . " Billy began, then hesitated. "Do you think that King Arthur really could come back to life, like Mr Parker said. You know, if England was invaded, or in danger or something?"

Keith thought about the question for a moment.

"No," he replied firmly.

"Why not?" Billy persisted. "He could be in a cave somewhere, *couldn't* he?"

"No." Keith shook his head. "King Arthur – well, he's part of history, right?"

Billy nodded.

"And history," Keith continued, "is all about dead people, right?"

Billy nodded again.

"So," concluded Keith, "he must be properly dead or he wouldn't be part of history, would he?"

As always, Keith's logic was flawless.

The two boys walked on in silence.

"I suppose you're right," Billy agreed reluctantly. "But it would be good, wouldn't it? I mean, if King Arthur and all his knights came back. Then we could have real swords and be *real* knights." He brandished his stick in the air, and slashed and stabbed at imaginary foes.

"Then we could fight dragons and monsters, and go on quests. Wouldn't that be great!"

"Yeah," agreed Keith. Then he frowned. "As long as we didn't have to do all that soppy stuff – you know, saving damsels in distress." Keith thought about the problem for a moment. "Of course, what we could do," he suggested, "is to let the dragons eat the damsels *first*, and then kill the dragons after. That way we wouldn't have to marry anybody."

The two boys were now walking beside the green-painted iron railings that surrounded All Souls Churchyard. The graveyard had the strongest fence of any place in the village. No one knew why. Nobody in the village was at all keen to get in, and none of the inhabitants of the graveyard had ever shown any signs of trying to get out.

The two boys began dragging their sticks along the railings: "Clacka-clacka-clacka-clacka . . . "

Mr Wilbury, the gardener, was just settling down on a gravestone for a well-earned nap. Beneath his broad shoulders were carved the words:

In blessed memory of Mary Ann Evans
Fell asleep, December 22, 1880
Aged 61 years

Under his even broader backside was a little poem:

Though memories fade and eyes grow dim,
We always will remember her.

It was Mr Wilbury's first day in his new job, and although he'd been mowing the grass since half past eight that morning the place *still* looked like a jungle.

"Never believe what you read in the papers," he muttered to himself. "Especially not the adverts."

Mr Wilbury's job had been advertised in *The Weekly Gazette*:

Part-time handyman/gardener wanted for
All Souls Church, Holebridge.
Light gardening and general maintenance.
10 hours a week.
Would suit fit and active pensioner.

Light gardening? What a joke! The grass in the western end of the churchyard was waist-high. He'd had to cut it with a scythe. He'd earned his forty winks, no doubt about it.

Mr Wilbury spread a large grimy handkerchief over his face to keep the sun out of his eyes. He was just beginning to doze off, when: "Clacka-clacka-clacka-clacka . . . "

He sat up, and lifted one corner of his handkerchief to see who was making that awful racket. Pesky kids! Typical!

"Oi! You two!" he yelled.

Billy and Keith heard the muffled shout and peered through the railings. The sound seemed to be coming from the west side of the church-yard. The sun was bright, but they could see a figure rising up from one of the old graves. It was wearing mud-stained moleskin trousers and an old-fashioned collarless shirt.

"What do you think you're playing at?" Mr Wilbury bellowed.

But the grubby handkerchief covered half his face and his mouth.

The blurred figure Billy and Keith saw rising from the grave with a halo of light behind it looked terrifying. Not only was it covered in soil, but the left side of its face was a blank, greyish-white – bare bone!

"Garf!" it yelled. "Wargh, wumpf – waaarf!"

"Aarrrgh!" shrieked the two boys.

"Woooaah!" yelled the dreadful figure, and it lifted up a hand and began to peel back its ghastly grey-white skull.

"It's – it's – a g-g-ghost!" screamed Keith.

"Oi!" yelled the awful spectre. "Come back!"

17

And it began to stride across the graveyard towards them.

"Leggit!" shrieked Keith, and the two boys dropped their sticks and sprinted off up the hill.

Mr Wilbury stopped and looked over the fence.

"Cheeky young varmints!" he thought. "Coming up here and yelling 'Ghost!' and then running away."

He grinned. He remembered when he'd been a boy of twelve, more than fifty years ago. His favourite game had been knocking on doors in the village and running away. "Knock down Ginger," he chuckled, and stuffed the grubby handkerchief back into his pocket.

He yawned and stretched. "Oh well, that's my nap ruined," he thought. "I might as well get some more work done." And he walked back towards the tool shed to get the scythe out again.

"No rest for the wicked," he muttered as he unlocked the shed door.

Three

Ever since Mr Parker had started reading the stories of King Arthur and the Knights of the Round Table, the normal playtime noises – the war-whoops of Red Indian braves and the hypnotic slap-slap of skipping ropes – had been drowned out by the neighing of horses and the cries of wounded knights. But next morning playtime at Holebridge School was unusually quiet. Most of the older children weren't playing any games at all; they were standing in a tight circle on the far side of the school field. In the centre of the circle stood Billy Simpkins and Keith Hall. They were telling the story of the ghost in the graveyard.

"So there we were, walking up the hill minding our own business," explained Billy, "when we heard these horrible moaning sounds coming from the graveyard. So we— "

"What were they like – these moaning sounds?" asked Matthew Evans. He always liked to get every detail clear in his mind.

"Well . . . like moaning," replied Keith. "You know, 'Wooooah!' That sort of thing."

"Yeah. Well, anyway," Billy continued,

19

anxious to get on with the story. "There we were, walking up the hill, when— "

"Whooooah? Like that?"

"Yes," said Billy impatiently. "So, there we were walking up— "

"Are you sure? Wooooah?"

"Yes!"

Billy wasn't the only one who was getting fed-up with Matthew's nit-picking.

"Shut up, Matthew."

"Let him get on with it."

"Nerrrgh! Typical Matthew."

Matthew decided to let the matter rest, for now. But he still wasn't happy about the ghost going "Whoooah!" The monsters in his horror comics always went "Waarrrgh!"

Billy started again. "So there we were, walking up the hill, when we heard this moaning." He shot a threatening glance at Matthew. "And we *saw* it. It was covered in mud and earth, and . . . it *didn't have a face* – just a skull, all white and shiny, like *bones*!"

Billy paused for a second. He looked round the circle of children. They were hanging on every word he said.

He carried on, "It started coming towards us – closer and closer and closer. Then, all of a sudden, it was running right at us! It tried to grab us – like this" – Billy lunged out with outstretched arms – "but we . . . er, fought it off and ran away."

Billy had to stop talking. He was breathless with excitement. Simply telling the story had been like reliving it. It was as if he could see the ghost, standing over him once again; he could almost feel its horrible, bony, skeletal fingers clutching at his sleeve!

All the children in the circle were silent, totally convinced. They *knew* Billy and Keith must have seen a real ghost. After all, they'd seen it in the graveyard; and it had moaned and groaned like a ghost should. Most convincing of all, it had tried to grab hold of them.

It was Matthew Evans who finally broke the silence.

"Was it a man ghost or a lady ghost?" he asked.

"It was a man," replied Keith, eager to share some of the glory. "He had trousers on. And he was really tall – like Frankenstein's monster – and he had big pointy teeth, and he . . . "

All the time Billy had been talking, Christine Robinson had stayed at the back of the group of children. She'd watched, helplessly, as Deirdre and Neelam had gradually edged their way closer and closer to the front – further and further away from her.

"Stupid boys, with their stupid stories about

stupid ghosts!" she'd muttered to herself, loud enough for the children in front of her to hear, though none of them had taken any notice of her.

But as Keith began to improve on the story of the ghost – pointed teeth, claws, fangs dripping with blood – Christine felt the first stirrings of doubt among some of the children. Keith had gone too far! Christine pounced.

"I don't believe you, Billy Simpkins – or you, Keith Hall," she announced in a clear, ringing voice. "I think it's all a great big fib. Monsters with big teeth like Frankenstein! I've been past that graveyard hundreds and hundreds of times, and *I've* never seen a ghost. I think you've made it all up. You're . . . you're . . . just copying all those stories Mr Parker's been telling us about knights fighting dragons and monsters. I think it's all a pack of lies!"

All eyes were now on Christine. She wasn't at the centre of the circle, but she was the centre of attention once more.

"And I think anyone who believes you," she continued, this time staring straight at Deirdre and Neelam, "must be really stupid! Everyone knows there's no such thing as ghosts. It's all a lie – a great big *lie!*"

"No it isn't!" snapped Billy. "It's all true, every word. You're just jealous, Christine Robinson, 'cos it wasn't you that saw it. Me and Keith saw a real ghost, so there!"

Billy looked around the circle of children, sure that all the others would join in on his side. He waited for someone to shout Christine down, to sneer at her the way she'd sneered at him.

There wasn't so much as a whisper from anyone, not even Keith!

Billy felt his rage swelling. It was a matter of honour: Christine had called him a liar! Where were his knights? Where was his King's Champion?

"It *is* true . . . " began Keith, but his voice sounded less firm and confident than before. Christine's outburst had caught him off-balance. He realised now that for the last few minutes he'd been improving the story. He couldn't be certain now whether he'd seen the huge pointy teeth or not. How much *had* he seen? Keith wasn't sure.

"All right, *if* it's true, prove it! Go on, show us some proof."

Billy looked at Keith. Keith looked at Billy. What could they say? They'd seen it, wasn't that enough? How could they prove that their story was true? Hadn't they told everyone about it, just as it happened . . . well, more or less?

"*See*, I told you so! It's all a big fib. There isn't

any stupid ghost in the graveyard. Go on, admit it, you just made it up to make yourselves look big!"

"No we didn't!" shouted Billy, going red in the face with anger. "There was a ghost in the graveyard, and we saw it!"

Christine pointed at Billy's scarlet cheeks.

"Oooooh, look," she shrieked, "he's going red, he's going red. Billy Simpkins is *blushing* – so it can't be true!"

No one spoke, but it was obvious from their faces that all of the girls and most of the boys were now convinced that Billy and Keith had made the whole thing up.

Every girl in the group knew that Christine was right. Boys *did* invent stories to make themselves look big; and they were always stories about fights and monsters and blood and guts – stuff that no girl would ever believe. Not like girls' stories. You could never tell with girls' stories whether they were true or not: "Brenda told me to tell you that she doesn't want to be your friend any more . . . ", "I saw Sarah's party list, and *you're* not on it . . . " However much blood got spilt in boys' stories, they were really just kids' stuff. They weren't about *real* pain and real suffering, like the stories girls told.

Billy was furious. "Right!" he yelled. "We'll

prove it – me and Keith – we'll show you. We'll show you, *Christine Robinson* . . . "

But Christine had already turned her back on him and was walking away. Deirdre and Neelam followed close behind.

"Any proof you like!" Billy shouted. "You just name it – go on, name it – and we'll get it."

Christine stopped walking. She turned to face Billy and the dwindling circle of children. The challenge was irresistible.

"A photograph," she said. "Show me a photograph of the ghost. Then I *might* believe you."

"Fine!" yelled Billy. "No problem! Easy! We'll get a photograph – yeah, we'll get one *tonight*. Then you'll be sorry, Christine-Smartypants-Robinson, then you'll be sorry!"

Four

O what can ail thee, knight at arms,
   Alone and palely loitering?
The sedge has withered from the lake,
   And no birds sing.

O what can ail thee, knight at arms,
   So haggard and so woe-begone?

Billy let the mournful words of the poem wash over him like black waves. Mr Parker had said it was a difficult poem, but Billy knew exactly how the knight felt, even if he didn't understand every single word. The doleful rhythm of the poem matched Billy's mood perfectly.

Billy let his head slump forward on to the table. Mr Parker's voice faded, until it was just an irregular hum in the background.

"We'll get a photograph," the voice in Billy's head repeated. "We'll get one *tonight*. Then you'll be sorry . . . then you'll be sorry . . . then you'll be sorry . . . "

Billy screwed his fists up tightly, and tried to make the mocking echo of his voice go away.

"Idiot!" he muttered to himself. "Numbskull, moron!"

Once again he'd let his big mouth get him into trouble. Once again he'd let Christine Robinson make a fool of him.

The same thing had happened a month ago, at the Junior Disco in the Church Hall – only it wasn't ghosts that time, it was snooker balls.

They'd had a big argument about whether it was possible to get a snooker ball into your mouth.

"It's impossible," Christine had said, "everybody knows that. It can't be done!"

"Bet it can," Billy had said.

"Can't!"

"Can!"

"Can't!"

"Can!"

"Can't!"

"Can!" And Billy had taken a red ball from the box on top of the upright piano and shoved it into his mouth. It hadn't been easy, but he'd done it.

"Gheee! Gunghd ick!" he'd announced proudly.

"That's the easy bit," Christine had smirked. "Now try and get it *out* – big mouth!"

And she was right! He'd stretched, and gagged, and tried to pull his jaws open . . . then Mr Wiggins, who ran the Youth Club tried . . . then Mrs Wiggins, who had done a Red Cross

First Aid course tried ... Finally they'd taken him to the Casualty Ward at the hospital.

"You're lucky it was only a half-size ball," the doctor had said. "If it had been a full-size ball we'd have had to take all your front teeth out and dislocate your jaw! How does it feel now?"

"Gnnnungggh!" Billy had replied. It felt as if he'd been kicked in the face by a horse.

"Good," the doctor had said. "I hope it hurts. It might teach you not to do stupid things like that in future."

And now, barely four weeks later, Christine had done it again. Billy was in trouble, and all because of Christine ...

Billy's thoughts were interrupted by a nudge from Keith. Billy looked up. Mr Parker hadn't stopped reading, but he was glaring fiercely in Billy's direction.

Billy took the hint. He sat up straight, and tried his best to listen to the rest of the poem:

I saw pale kings and princes too,
    Pale warriors, death-pale were they all;
Who cried, "La Belle Dame sans Merci
    Hath thee in thrall!"

Billy looked at Keith and shrugged his shoulders. Which kings and princes? Why were they pale? And what was a "thrall"? Billy

had missed so much of the poem that he didn't know what was going on any more.

"She's poisoned them," whispered Keith. "And the knight, too – poisoned beetroot and wild honey!" And he made a face like someone being violently sick.

Billy giggled.

"Sssshh!" Mr Parker pointed a threatening finger at Billy and Keith, and carried on reading:

And I awoke and found me here
    On the cold hill's side.

And this is why I sojourn here
    Alone and palely loitering,
Though the sedge is withered from the lake,
    And no birds sing.

Mr Parker let out a long, dramatic sigh and closed the book. He seemed to have enjoyed the poem a lot. But Billy felt disappointed, cheated. He'd been hoping that the knight would go after the Bell Damn woman and cut her into little pieces with his sword. The ending had been a real let-down: *Then I woke up!* "Even I could do better than that," thought Billy.

"I hope you all managed to follow what was going on in that poem," Mr Parker said. "It was very like some of the stories of King Arthur.

Maybe the poet was thinking of Morgan Le Fay when he wrote it . . . ?" There was an awkward silence. It was clear from the expressions on the children's faces that they hadn't enjoyed the poem very much.

"Well, now," continued Mr Parker brightly, "has anyone got any questions about the poem – anything you didn't understand?"

There was an even longer silence. Eventually, a hand went up.

"Yes, Matthew?"

"Please, Mr Parker, what kind of birds were they?"

Mr Parker looked puzzled. "I'm sorry, Matthew, I don't know what you mean."

"The birds, Mr Parker," Matthew repeated. "What sort of birds were they?"

Mr Parker shook his head. He still didn't understand. "Birds . . . ?"

"The birds in the poem, sir," explained Matthew. "The birds that were singing: the *Know* Birds. What sort of birds are they, Mr Parker . . . ?"

Mr Parker sat down at his table and put his head in his hands.

Billy and Keith sat on the edge of the long-jump pit in silence. Occasionally one of them would jab at the sand with his stick. Both were thinking about the graveyard, and the photograph of the ghost they'd promised to take.

"Keith?"

"Yeah?"

"I was just thinking . . . " Billy began, then stopped.

"What?"

"Well, I was just thinking – what do you think would happen if we *didn't* go to the graveyard? Suppose we were . . . sick, or something, and couldn't go . . . ?"

Keith waggled his stick in its sandy scabbard. "But we're not, are we?" he said. He shook his head. "We can't back out now. We can't. We said we'd get a picture to prove it. If we don't get a photo nobody'll ever believe anything we say – ever again!"

Both Billy and Keith knew that the worst thing in the world was to be branded a liar. Nobody wanted to play with a liar; nobody wanted to be your friend if they could never believe what you said. It was worse than being stupid, it was even worse than being smelly.

"I know," said Billy. "But remember how it yelled at us – and that was in the day. What if it *really* tried to grab us? I mean, it's bound to be worse when it's dark, isn't it? And we haven't got a camera, either – at least, not one that'll work in the dark."

Billy had an old Kodak Brownie that had once belonged to his mum, but it was twenty years old. It didn't have a flash, and Billy wasn't even sure whether it had any film in it.

Without warning, Keith leapt to his feet with a yell. "Of course!" he shouted. *"Ron!"*

"Ron?" Billy looked up at him, totally confused.

"Yeah!" yelled Keith, dancing round Billy in excitement. "My brother Ron! He's got a brilliant camera! It's one of those special ones – Instantwotsits – that makes the picture come out as soon as you've taken it, *and* it's got a flash! And when he was on holiday in Switzerland with the army cadets he took all these dead good pictures of mountains!"

"Mountains?"

"Yeah! Don't you see? Those mountains were like miles and miles away. So if you can take pictures of something miles and miles away with Ron's camera – like mountains – it'll be dead easy taking a picture of the ghost. We probably won't even have to go into the graveyard at all! We'll be able to take a picture from the other side of the road, and he won't even know we're there!"

Billy leapt to his feet, too. It was a brilliant idea! Good old Keith! Billy felt his spirits soar. Everything would be all right after all, Billy was sure. Yes! They'd get the photo and everyone would believe them. They'd be heroes!

They might even get a medal for being so brave.

Billy bent down and picked up his sword from the sand-pit. He held it aloft.

"And it'll be our quest," he declared. "Our very own quest, just like the Knights of the Round Table."

Keith stooped and picked up his sword.

"It'll be like Sir Gawain and the Green Knight," Billy continued, "or the Quest for The Grail. This'll be our chance to be like real knights."

Billy paused for a moment. When he spoke again his voice was calm and solemn. "I think we should swear an oath or something before we go home, just like knights did before they went off to kill dragons and things."

He tried to remember. What exactly did knights do before they went off to be brave and fearless? Then he remembered something from an old adventure movie.

"I know," he said. "We'll raise our swords and say, 'One for all and all for one!' Okay?"

Keith nodded.

The two boys held up their sticks and shouted, "One for all and all for— "

"Hey, you two! Billy and Keith! What do you think you're doing?"

It was Mr Fairbrother striding across the field towards them. His face was very stern.

"This is the second day running that I've come out here – long after you're supposed to have gone home – and found you two playing wild games with sticks. Don't you realise how dangerous it is?"

He stared hard at the two boys, who looked down at their feet.

"How many times," Mr Fairbrother continued, "do you have to be told something before you'll take the slightest notice?"

Billy and Keith said nothing.

"I suppose you were just 'messing about' again, were you? Well?"

"Dunno, sir," replied Billy.

Mr Fairbrother made a noise like an angry kettle just coming to the boil. "Yesterday afternoon – not last month, or last year, but *yesterday* – I reminded you that it was against school rules to play any games after school unless there was a teacher with you. I also reminded you that you must *not* play with sticks. That was a friendly warning, but you've completely ignored it. Well, what have you got to say for yourselves?"

Billy and Keith kept staring at the ground. Keith shook his head.

"Yes, Keith? Were you about to say something?"

"Er . . . I'm sorry, Mr Fairbrother."

"I'm afraid sorry isn't good enough this time, Keith. Both of you seem to have forgotten that

I'm in charge of this school. That means that if anything goes wrong, if one of you gets badly hurt for example, I'm the one who gets the blame. I can't do my job properly if children simply ignore everything I, or the other teachers, say. We have rules in this school to protect you, Billy and Keith; to prevent you doing silly things that might injure you or someone else. And it seems to me that if you two can't be trusted to behave sensibly, even after being reminded, then I'll have to make sure that your memories improve. Perhaps some punishment – maybe losing your playtimes for a week – will help you remember what I tell you in future.

"I think you ought to go home now – and I mean straight home! We'll talk about this again tomorrow. Come and see me in the morning, after assembly."

Five

Billy trudged up the hill alone. He felt weary and fed-up. The excitement he'd felt only a short while before had vanished. Just as everything seemed about to turn out all right, Mr Fairbrother had appeared and Billy's new-found optimism had been squashed.

"It isn't fair," thought Billy. "Why does everything I do always go wrong?" He never went looking for trouble, and yet it always seemed to be waiting for him round the next corner, ready to pounce. And it wasn't his fault. He and Keith hadn't been doing anything wrong – they certainly hadn't been fighting. They were best friends, surely Mr Fairbrother knew that.

Suddenly, Billy heard the snap of a dry twig. The sound came from somewhere to his right. Then Billy heard the rustle of branches and leaves. Slowly Billy realised that he was standing outside the graveyard.

The graveyard!

Billy felt the tiny hairs on the back of his neck stand up. He felt a rippling chill run up his back. He didn't turn round, he didn't even swivel his eyes, but he *knew* that someone was watching him from behind the churchyard fence. He knew that someone, or something, was just the other side of the iron railings and creeping closer and closer and closer . . .

Billy didn't stop running until he'd reached the top of the hill.

He flopped down on the vicarage wall, struggling to get his breath back. He was sweating, panicking. He tried to control his fear. It was stupid, behaving like this. It was the middle of the afternoon and the sun was shining brightly. He could hear the sound of music coming through an open window of the vicarage. He knew that just round the corner, in his street, mums and dads would be weeding their front gardens; little kids would be trundling up and down the pavement on their tricycles; and big kids would be doing whatever it was that big kids did underneath old motorcycles and clapped-out cars.

Billy was surrounded by noise, people, safety. And yet he was running away in terror from the thing in the graveyard. So what would it be like tonight, Billy thought, at midnight, when he and Keith went into the graveyard all alone?

"Are you *sure* you're feeling all right, Billy?" asked his mum, for the umpteenth time that night.

She leaned across the table and, once again, pressed her palm against Billy's forehead. It was cool, just like before.

"Well, at least you haven't got a temperature – *yet*. But you've been looking peaky ever since you came in from school." She pursed her lips and frowned. "What do you think, Eileen? Do you think he looks okay?"

Billy's big sister Eileen didn't answer immediately. She was eating pickled onions. She impaled her seventh on the pickle fork and popped it into her mouth. Crunch! First things first, and with Eileen food always came first. Eventually she glanced at Billy.

"No worse than usual," she replied. "Nothing that a good hosing down and five or six years of plastic surgery couldn't put right."

"Oh, ha-ha-ha!" Billy tried to do his sarcastic laugh, but it just came out sounding weak and weedy.

Billy's mum looked down at his plate: this was no joking matter. Billy's Cornish pasty and chips lay cooling on his plate, barely fiddled with.

"Well, I don't know . . . " she frowned again, trying to remember something. "Billy?"

"Yes, Mum."

"Didn't Keith Hall have chicken-pox a couple of weeks ago?"

Billy tried to work out what she was talking

about. Keith had never been ill in his entire life.

Slowly the pieces fitted together. "No, Mum. That was Keith *Fletcher*. And anyway, it wasn't chicken-pox. It was something in his mum's washing powder, it made him come out in spots. He was – whatsit – anaemic to it."

Eileen sniggered. "Oughf greenf arrejickgh!" She choked and swallowed her ninth pickled onion whole.

"That'll teach you not to speak with your mouth full," scolded their mother, as she thumped Eileen on the back. "I know what he means: allergic."

But Mrs Simpkins wasn't convinced, not for a minute. Chicken-pox was the obvious explanation. It couldn't be a coincidence. She stared at Billy long and hard, as if she expected to see spots pop up at any moment.

Six

After tea, Billy and his mum and Eileen went into the living room to watch TV.

They were just in time for the first episode of a new comedy series called *Sorry, Darling, It's All My Fault*. It was all about a weedy, silly little man who seemed to be surrounded by big, tough women who were always bullying him. Usually Billy didn't like those sorts of programmes, but tonight he didn't mind. It was a relief to have his mum staring at the TV instead of staring at him.

But as the plot got sillier and sillier, Billy got more and more bored and fidgety.

"Do keep still, Billy," his mother nagged. "I'm trying to watch this." Then she added, "Watch this bit. I saw it on the trailer last night – it's ever so funny!"

Billy tried his hardest to keep still. On the screen, the silly little man was trying to put up a shelf in his kitchen. It was a disaster. In less than five minutes his tie got caught in his electric drill, he dropped his hammer on his foot, and he nailed his left thumb to the wall. Then, when the shelf appeared to be up at last, it fell down on his head and knocked him out.

The studio audience hooted with laughter.

Good, thought Billy, that must be the end. But it wasn't. The last scene was in hospital. The silly little man was trying to reach a bunch of grapes his awful wife had brought him and left on his bedside table. He fell out of bed and broke his arm.

The audience howled with laughter and applauded wildly.

"God! I don't know why you watch such rubbish," sneered Eileen, as soon as the show was over. "It was awful!"

"Well, *I* thought it was funny," declared Mrs Simpkins. "Mind you," she added, "it's hard to enjoy anything with Billy wriggling around as if he's got ants in his pants . . . Which reminds me, how are you feeling now, Billy?"

But Billy didn't answer. He was miles away, imagining what would be happening in only a few hours' time. The same pictures kept appearing in his head, over and over again, like scenes in a horror film: the blackened graveyard; an owl hooting; two small boys walking through the huge iron gates; the awful shape rising up from out of the ground . . .

"*Billy!* I'm talking to you. I said, Do you feel all right?"

His mother's voice cut through the nightmare.

The dreadful visions vanished, and he was back in his living room again.

"What? Oh, yes. Yes, I'm all right, Mum."

"Well, you don't look well to me. You've gone all pale. What do you think, Eileen? Don't you think he looks pale? Eileen?"

But Eileen was completely lost in the wonderful, romantic world of a chocolate bar commercial. Glamorous women in swirling silk ball-gowns were floating up and down the corridors of a dimly lit palace munching creamy chocolate bars. It was Eileen's idea of heaven.

Mrs Simpkins snorted with exasperation. "I don't know what I'm going to do with you two! I'd do better having a conversation with the sofa than to try and talk to you when that thing's on . . . Oooh, good, it's the holiday programme on next. Now, not a word from either of you until it's over – and Billy, no more fidgeting please."

But as the opening music began, Billy got to his feet.

"Actually, Mum," he said in a low voice, "I think I'll go up to my room for a bit. I've got . . . er . . . stuff to get ready for school tomorrow."

As Billy plodded upstairs, Mrs Simpkins hissed at Eileen in her loudest whisper, "You mark my words, he'll be covered in spots by the morning!"

"I'm sure that boy's sickening for something . . . George? *George!* Did you hear me? This is import-ant, so listen."

Billy's dad grunted, but didn't open his eyes. It had been a long, tiring day at the Fire Station. Besides, he always listened much better with his eyes closed.

"George, wake up! I'm worried about him. He hardly touched his tea, and he's been moping around like a wet weekend all evening. *And* he went straight to bed – no excuses, no arguments. That isn't like Billy at all. I'm sure it's chicken-pox."

"Well, if you say it's chicken-pox I'm sure you're right."

Billy's mother gave a grumpy "Hummmph".

Billy's dad yawned and stretched. "Well, love," he said sleepily, "I'm on early watch tomorrow. I think I'm ready for bed. How about you?"

Billy's mother nodded, still peeved.

George Simpkins stood up and began his nightly routine of pulling out all the plugs and double-checking the gas cooker and the gas fires. (The gas fires hadn't been lit for more than a month, but he still checked them, just to make sure.) His wife stood in the doorway, tapping her fingers impatiently on the door jamb.

"Okay," he thought, "so I'm fussy, so what?" He had been a fireman for sixteen years. He knew what could happen when people *weren't* fussy.

As his wife clomped up the stairs, George began double-checking that all the downstairs doors were closed. Neurotic? So what? Who wouldn't be, if they'd been called out to as many house fires as Billy's dad.

Billy lay in his bed, dripping with sweat – but it wasn't the first sign of chicken-pox. Under his pyjamas Billy was wearing his jeans, shirt, sweater, thick socks and anorak. He was clutching his torch in one hand and his trainers in the other. As soon as his parents were asleep he'd be off – off to that awful graveyard. Just him and Keith. In the dark. All alone. Even the thought of that couldn't cool Billy down.

He heard the creak of the loose floorboards outside his room. His parents were standing outside his door listening.

Billy pulled the duvet over his head and started to snore. A moment later he heard a sharp intake of breath, and then his mother's triumphant whisper: "See? What did I tell you? Tonsillitis! Did you hear that breathing? I knew I was right, it's definitely tonsillitis."

Their footsteps moved across the landing. Billy

could hear his father's puzzled voice: "But I thought you said it was chicken-pox . . . "

"That's not important," Billy's mother replied impatiently. "I knew he was sickening for *something*, I knew it!"

Billy listened to the clanks, gargles and gushes as his parents got ready for bed. Then everything went quiet.

Billy counted slowly up to two hundred.

"Please," he thought. "Please, please make a noise. Please make it so I can't go."

Nothing. Not a single sound.

He counted up to two hundred again, even more slowly – just to make sure, just to give them a second chance . . . No. Not a single creaking floorboard, not a single muffled footstep. Billy could even hear the soft whistle of his mother's breathing, followed by the unmistakable snore which she refused to believe she made. They were asleep, no doubt about it.

Wretchedly, Billy slipped out of bed and laced up his shoes. He tiptoed out of his room and across the landing. He crept downstairs, through the empty hall, to the front door.

He stopped at the front door. One last chance for them to stop him. *Please?*

It was no good. Billy let himself quietly out of the front door.

* * *

46

But upstairs, George Simpkins was awake.

It was always the same; no matter how tired he was, if he dozed off downstairs he could never get to sleep once he got to bed. And now he was worrying about the plugs.

Did he pull out the TV plug? Yes.

Are you sure? he asked himself. Yes.

Really sure? Yes.

Absolutely, completely, utterly, one hundred per cent sure? Er . . .

It was no good. He'd have to get up and check them all over again or he'd lie awake for hours worrying. He put on his dressing gown and slipped silently out of the bedroom.

"Funny," he thought. "Billy's door . . . it's open."

He walked quickly across the landing. Something wasn't right. He didn't know what, but he could sense that something wasn't right.

He looked into Billy's room. Even with the light off he could see the duvet thrown back, the empty bed.

"Billy must be up," he thought. "I hope he's not feeling ill."

Then he realised what it was that had felt wrong: Billy wasn't in his room, but the house was silent. Billy *always* made a dreadful racket if he got up in the night.

He went to the top of the landing and looked

down the stairwell into the hall. No lights. No sound, except for his own breathing getting faster.

He ran downstairs – into the living room, the kitchen, the dining room – snapping on the lights. No Billy!

Now he felt it – like icy waves breaking over him – fear! The fear no mother or father will dare to name.

George Simpkins ran back up the stairs, completely unaware that he was shouting at the top of his voice.

Seven

Billy scuttled down the road in a half-crouching, commando-style run. He darted from lamppost to lamppost; from one pool of light to the next.

The road was deserted. As Billy reached the fourth lamppost the church clock began to strike the quarter-hour – a quarter to midnight.

Billy peered ahead, but he couldn't see any sign of Keith. His heart sank; what if Keith wasn't coming? What if Keith's mum or dad had caught him trying to sneak out?

"What if I'm out here," thought Billy, "in the dark, all alone?"

He dodged to the next lamppost, and paused to get his breath back. Then he dodged to the next. From here, Billy could see the corner of the road; and he could just make out a dark figure, lurking in the darker shadows of the scruffy hedge that surrounded the vicarage.

Billy fumbled for the button on his torch: two short flashes, that was the signal. Billy waited for a reply. Instead, from the shadows came a faint crash, and the tinkling sound of broken glass, followed by the noise of someone scrabbling about on hands and knees. It was Keith.

Billy crossed the road and hurried to the corner. As Billy got closer the sight of Keith in his dark blue anorak and SAS balaclava made Billy feel more cheerful. Maybe it wouldn't be so bad after all. Maybe they'd get a picture and get away without any trouble. Perhaps they wouldn't see the ghost at all. Perhaps it was only a daytime ghost and didn't come out at night. Whatever happened, even if they didn't get a photo at all, nobody could say they hadn't tried.

By the time Billy reached the corner Keith was standing up again.

"I dropped my torch," Keith explained. "I think the bulb's bust." And he shook the torch. It rattled ominously. "But I've got the camera."

Keith unzipped the front of his anorak and pulled out a large, squarish object.

"It's got a flash – like I told you – and it can take pictures from all different distances. I've brought the instruction book too, but I set it on *Maximum Distance* before I left home. But whatever you do, don't mention it in front of my brother Ron. He'd kill me if he ever found out I'd borrowed his camera."

Billy shone his torch on the camera. It was a lot more complicated than he'd expected. There were four dials around the lens, each with a different set of coloured numbers and symbols; and

51

Billy could see at least three different buttons.

"How does it work?" Billy asked.

"Easy – you just aim it, and press this red button here."

"Like this?"

There was a sudden explosion of blinding white light.

The two boys leapt backwards into the hedge.

They waited for the inevitable shouts, the sounds of running feet . . .

The only sound was a soft *Whirrr-click* from the camera.

"Billy," whispered Keith, after a second or two. "Shine the torch down here – I think something's happening!"

Billy switched the torch on again, and shone it on to the camera. Sticking out of the bottom was a square, stubby tongue.

Keith pulled it out and peeled off the top layer. As the two boys watched, a ghostly image began to appear on the white square.

"What is it?" Billy whispered.

Two blurred white shapes, like eyeless fish, appeared on the picture. They seemed to be swimming in a murky pool of pale grey soup.

"I think it's my feet," replied Keith, also in a whisper. He studied the picture for a second or two, and then stuffed it into the pocket of his anorak.

"But that only leaves two more pictures on the film," he hissed, "so be careful! Come on, let's get going . . . before we lose any more."

Keeping very close together, they started to creep down the hill towards the graveyard.

The night was silent and moonless. As the two boys made their way down the unlit hill the darkness seemed to thicken and take on a substance all of its own, like the dense black breath of some vast coiled beast. The thin beam of the torch only made the surrounding darkness seem all the more menacing and dreadful.

Suddenly, Keith froze.

"What was that?"

Billy snapped off the torch.

The two boys held their breath, listening.

"Did you hear it?" whispered Keith.

"What?"

"A sort of scratching sound."

The two boys listened again.

All around them they could sense bodiless creatures gathering in the darkness. Any moment, the silence would burst with terrible shrieks and cries . . .

But no sound came. Not even a breeze stirred the leaves of the yew trees overhead.

"Ah!" Billy just managed to strangle a yell. Something warm and soft had rubbed against his right ankle.

"Keith!" he gasped. "It's . . . it's . . . "

"Miaaooow!"

Billy let out a low groan as the vicar's tabby cat rubbed itself against his other leg.

"Scram!" Keith hissed ferociously.

The cat purred, and rolled over on to its back to have its tummy tickled.

They were still ten metres from the gates of the churchyard.

"Come on," whispered Keith, stepping round the contented cat. "We can't give up now."

Slowly the two boys inched their way down the hill.

The graveyard had been swallowed up by the darkness. The laurel shrubs, the gravestones and the two carved stone angels had vanished. There was nothing behind the iron railings but a limit-less black void filled with unnameable horrors. The two boys shrank back from the iron gates, appalled by the total darkness beyond.

Finally, Billy whispered, "G-g-go on, Keith. You go first, you've got the camera."

Keith didn't move. "N-no, you go first. You've got the torch."

Billy's heart began to race, faster and faster. Keith was right, he would have to go first.

Billy took a step forward . . .

He closed his eyes . . .

He stretched out a trembling hand . . .

He pushed . . .

Creeek – clunk! The gate stuck.

He pushed again, harder.

There was a rattling, clanking sound and the gate stuck again, and wouldn't budge.

Billy stepped back and shone the torch beam at the gates.

He let out a great sigh of relief.

"It's no good," he whispered. "Look . . . "

A thick chain was wrapped around the gates, and it was secured by a huge padlock.

The two boys stared up at the chain and lock, and at the gates – they were much too high to climb.

"I suppose . . . we could climb over the fence?" suggested Keith.

Billy moved the torch beam sideways, across the iron railings. There were no obvious handholds or footholds, and the pointed spikes on the top of each iron post glinted viciously in the pale light.

Neither boy wanted to be the first to say, "Let's give up and go home."

Bong!

Billy nearly jumped out of his skin as the first chime rang out.

Bong! Bong! Bong!

The darkness pulsated with the heavy clang of the church clock striking midnight.

Bong! Bong! Bong! Bong!

Keith had his hands over his ears – the sound was deafening after the silence.

Bong! Bong! Bong! Bong!

Billy gave a sigh of relief. That was the last chime: twelve. He gave Keith a thumbs-up sign.

Bong!

Billy felt his knees go weak.

Thirteen! The church clock had struck *thirteen*: the summons for the undead to rise up and . . .

"Oi! You two!"

A shout rang out from up the hill.

Billy dropped his torch in terror.

"Stay where you are!" The voice yelled again. Then came the clatter of running feet.

"It's him!" shrieked Billy. "He's got out! He's coming to get us!"

Howling with fright, the two boys tore off down the hill.

"Come back!" yelled the voice again, louder and closer.

"Noooo!" screamed Billy. "Go away!"

The pounding feet got closer and closer.

"Stop!" yelled the voice.

"Leave us alone!" wailed Keith.

A huge, black shape lunged at Billy and Keith from behind.

"Right!" rasped the voice, as big hairy hands grabbed the two boys by their collars. "Gotcha!"

They struggled and squirmed, but their attacker was too strong for them. They tried to scream, but they were being choked by the iron grip of the awful monster. They were dragged – still wriggling and twisting – under the light of the street-lamp at the bottom of the hill.

They looked up, expecting to see the face of the ghastly ghost. Instead, to their horror, they found themselves gazing up into the crimson, furious face of PC Payne.

"Right, you two hooligans," he bellowed. "You're *nicked*!"

Eight

Billy and Keith stood in Mr Fairbrother's room – heads bowed, staring at the carpet.

"Well? I'm still waiting. What have you got to say for yourselves?"

Billy and Keith said nothing.

Mr Fairbrother was a patient man, but he was rapidly running out of patience with Billy and Keith.

"All right, then," he said, "let's run through what you've been up to over the past two days, shall we?

"First of all, there's your disobedience. You deliberately ignored my warning not to fight with sticks, and not to play on the field after school without supervision.

"Then, just before assembly this morning, I received a telephone call from PC Payne. According to him, you two were prowling the streets last night, armed with a torch and a camera, up to goodness-knows-what! He also told me that you two put up quite a struggle when he tried to stop you.

"What *is* the matter with you two? Well?"

Once more Billy and Keith didn't answer.

"For heaven's sake! You've been standing there for nearly a quarter of an hour and I still haven't had a single word of explanation from either of you.

"Billy, you tell me – what's got into the pair of you?"

Billy shuffled awkwardly from foot to foot.

"I dunno, sir."

Standing in Mr Fairbrother's room, with the sun streaming through the window, made the events of last night seem unreal. Billy felt strangely remote from the whole adventure, as if it had all happened to someone else – a character in a film or a TV programme – and had nothing to do with the normal, everyday world of school and teachers and spelling and trying to get your sums right.

"*Dunno, sir?*" snapped Mr Fairbrother. "Is that the best you can do?"

He took a deep breath and counted to ten, trying to control his temper.

"Look," he began again, in a calmer voice this time, "you two aren't the naughtiest boys in the school – not usually – but over the past two days there hardly seems to have been a minute when you haven't been causing trouble of some kind."

Mr Fairbrother looked across at Billy and Keith. They were still gazing at the floor.

"For the moment, let's forget about the fighting with sticks and messing about after school," he suggested. "What concerns me much more is what you were up to last night. PC Payne told me that you were obviously scared out of your wits when he tried to stop you. He said you seemed to be running away from someone – or, rather, that you thought someone or something was chasing after you. Was it something to do with a fight? Were you expecting some sort of ambush? Is there some kind of gang-warfare going on in this school that I don't know anything about? You'd better tell me now if there is. Well?"

"No, sir," Billy said. "It wasn't anything . . . I mean, there wasn't any gang, or fighting, Mr Fairbrother."

"So . . . ?" Mr Fairbrother waited for a fuller explanation, but Billy just stared down at his feet again. These boys are hiding something, thought Mr Fairbrother, but what?

"Well then, what can you tell me about the camera?" asked Mr Fairbrother. He paused, then continued in a much sterner voice, "We've had this sort of thing happen before – with boys at this school – snooping round after dark, trying to look in other people's windows. It's a horrible thing to do, and if that's what you two were doing—"

"No, Mr Fairbrother! It wasn't that – honestly, it wasn't!" Billy blurted out. "We weren't trying to take pictures of anyone . . . well, I mean, not *living* people . . . that is . . . what I mean is . . ." Billy stuttered and stopped, his cheeks scarlet with embarrassment and confusion.

"Go on, Billy, what *were* you trying to take pictures of?"

"The graveyard, sir. We were trying to take pictures of the graveyard."

"In the middle of the night! Are you both out of your minds? It was pitch-black last night." Mr Fairbrother was starting to get really angry. The one thing he couldn't bear was children lying to him, and this was a transparent whopper!

"But we had a flash, sir," Keith added, nervously.

"I don't care if you had floodlights, a full camera crew and a fifty-piece orchestra to provide the background music!" Mr Fairbrother snapped. He noticed Billy and Keith flinch. "Don't shout," he muttered to himself. "Don't shout . . . stay calm . . . shouting never does any good."

"The point," he explained, through clenched teeth, "is not whether you were or were not equipped for night photography. What I want to know is, *what* were you trying to photograph?

And, to say the least, I find your story about trying to take a snap of the graveyard a little hard to believe."

"It was a ghost, sir," mumbled Billy, in a barely audible whisper.

"Say that again, Billy – louder, so I can be sure I heard you correctly."

"We thought we might – well, we thought there was a ghost in the graveyard."

Mr Fairbrother gave a long sigh. So that was it! It all made sense now: the graveyard . . . the camera . . . the panic of the two boys when PC Payne had grabbed them. It must be at least a year, thought Mr Fairbrother, since the last outbreak of ghost-fever – but that had been on the Fourth Year School Journey to Norfolk. This was the first case he could remember of a home-grown spook. He was just grateful that only two children were involved. Normally, as he knew, ghost-fever was more infectious than measles or chicken-pox. It was like hula-hoops, yo-yos, and flicking paper pellets with rubber bands. Whole classes got swept up in the latest craze.

However, he wasn't going to let Billy and Keith see his relief.

"That doesn't excuse your behaviour," he continued, as sternly as before. "I know your poor parents were worried sick – especially

62

yours, Billy. It was your father, wasn't it, who called PC Payne in the first place?"

Billy nodded solemnly, ashamed at the memory of his father's misery and his mother's tight-lipped anger.

"It was a very stupid thing to do – disappearing like that, in the middle of the night, without a word to anyone.

"And there's also the trouble you caused PC Payne. What if some serious crime had been committed last night, while PC Payne was chasing round the streets after you two? You have both been thoughtless, selfish, and very silly. I hope you realise that – do you?"

"Yes, sir."

"Yes, Mr Fairbrother."

"I understand PC Payne's already said a few words to you, is that correct?"

Billy and Keith nodded, glumly.

"And what should you be doing at the moment? What lesson are you missing?"

"English, sir," replied Billy.

"To make up for your missing English, you will spend playtime writing a letter each to PC Payne, apologising for all the bother you caused last night. *And* you can pay for the stamps. Now, you've got work to do, and so have I – so, go back to your lessons . . . Oh, and I want to see those letters before you give them to Mrs

Wentworth for posting. Any blots, smudges or spelling mistakes, and you'll write them out all over again. Is that clear?"

"Yes, sir."

"Yes, sir."

As the door closed, Mr Fairbrother looked at his watch: 10.15. He felt exhausted, but he hadn't managed to get any work done yet. He stared at the pile of paperwork on his desk: bills to be paid for new school library books; a coach to be booked for the Fourth Year School Journey (they were going to a bright, modern Youth Hostel in Derbyshire this year); an estimate for new guttering for the kitchens . . . Mr Fairbrother shuffled through the pile. And finally . . . Oh, no!

Right at the bottom of the pile, still uncorrected, were last week's dinner-money forms.

"I'll do them first thing this afternoon," Mr Fairbrother promised himself. "First thing this afternoon."

Nine

"See, see – I told you so!" Christine Robinson was almost dancing with jubilation. She'd had to wait until dinnertime to confront Billy and Keith, but for Christine it was a pleasure worth waiting for. She was now enjoying herself enormously.

"Go on, admit it, it was all a pack of lies from the start, wasn't it?"

"Go on, admit it!" sneered Deirdre and Neelam.

"I ain't afraid of no ghosts!" chorused all three girls together, and they shrieked with laughter.

Billy's face was scarlet with rage; Keith's fists were clenched.

"You would – *too* – have been scared," shouted Billy. "You wouldn't dare go into that graveyard – I bet! I bet you wouldn't go in there for . . . for . . . a million pounds!"

"I'm not scared of any stupid old graveyard!"

"Are!"

"Aren't!"

"Are!"

"I'm not afraid of *anything*, Billy Simpkins!"

"Are!"

"Aren't!"

"Are!"

"Aren't!"

Keith had been scraping at the loose earth at the edge of the long-jump pit. He stood up, with his hands behind his back.

"Here," he said, "I bet you're afraid of *this*," and he held out a huge pinky-grey earthworm and waggled it in front of Christine's face.

"Eeeeeeeergh!" she shrieked.

"See!" shouted Billy. "Scaredy-cat! Scaredy-cat! Cowardy-cowardy-custard!"

Keith dropped the worm back on to the crumbling earth.

"You're just a wet, soppy girl!" Billy hooted. "You wouldn't dare go into the graveyard like me and Keith did!"

"Would!"

"Wouldn't!"

"Would!"

"Prove it . . . "

All afternoon Mr Parker was interrupted by the twitterings of whispered messages, as the children in his class passed the news from one to another.

The sun came dazzling through the leaves,
And flamed upon the bronzen greaves
    Of bold Sir Lancelot . . .

66

"*Pssst!* Matthew, graveyard, after school. Billy and Keith and Christine are going to catch the ghost – pass it on."

"Matthew! Neelam! Pay attention – 'A red-cross knight for ever kneeled'."

"*Pssst!* Be at the graveyard this afternoon. Billy and Keith are going to kill a ghost – pass it on."

" 'As he rode down to Camelot . . . ' "

"*Pssst!* Graveyard, this afternoon – there's going to be a fight! Billy and Keith! Pass it on."

" 'And as he rode his armour rung . . . ' "

"*Pssst!*"

Mr Parker snapped the book closed. "Right, if you won't be quiet and listen," he retorted, "we'll have a spelling test! Rough books and pencils."

"Oh, Mr Parker . . . "

"Oh no, sir. It's not fair." The protests came thick and fast. "We *were* listening, Mr Parker – honest!"

At three-thirty, instead of the usual handful of children that normally turned left out of the school gates and walked up the hill past the church, thirty-two children – all of Class Four – began the long climb. No one wanted to miss out on the fun.

As the procession reached the church gates the other children hung back, waiting to see what Billy, Keith and Christine would do.

Billy looked all around. Apart from the crowd of children there was no one about; the church-yard was deserted, except for the marble head-stones and the two carved angels.

"Go on, then," he whispered to Christine. "If you're so brave, you go first."

"Why? What's the matter?" asked Christine, also whispering. "Are you frightened to go in first?"

"I tell you what," hissed Keith. "We'll all go in together, right?"

"Right!" whispered Billy and Christine together. Nobody moved.

"Okay, when I count three," suggested Keith. "One . . . Two . . . Three!"

As the three children crept through the gates the other twenty-nine fanned out along the fence. Faces pressed against the railings and peered out from behind bushes; no one wanted to miss a thing.

As she tiptoed along the gravel path Christine felt her confidence return. She could see that the graveyard was deserted, and she felt annoyed at herself for not being braver, for not marching straight up the path and really showing up those stupid boys!

She waited until they were right in the middle of the graveyard, then she stopped. Ignoring Billy and Keith, she turned to face the audience of eager faces peeping through the fence.

"See!" she announced in her loudest voice. "I told you so. There's nothing here at all – no ghost, *nothing!*"

Then she turned away from the fence and faced the two boys. She stuck out her tongue and chanted, "Nerh-nerh-nee-nerh-nerh – Billy is a li-er!"

A burly figure in brown moleskin trousers and an old-fashioned collarless shirt suddenly materialised by the side of the church.

"Oi!" he yelled. "What are you lot playing at?"

And he started to run towards the three startled children.

"*You* again!" he bellowed as he saw Billy and Keith.

"It's him!" shouted Keith. "It's . . . *the ghost!*"

The three children dashed down the path, squealing with fright. All the faces disappeared from between the railings, as the spectators started running away down the hill . . . all except one.

"No, no – *no!*" screamed Matthew Evans as the dreadful ghost pounded over the grass towards him. "Don't hurt me – don't kill me – don't eat me!" he sobbed.

He struggled desperately to free himself, but it was no good. His head was jammed firmly between the iron railings.

"Help!" he screamed as the ghost got closer and closer. *"Help! . . . "*

Ten

Mr Fairbrother strode down the corridor, his face dark with anger. When he arrived at the door of Mr Parker's classroom he didn't knock or even pause, he simply swept into the room.

"Sorry to interrupt your lesson, Mr Parker, but I want to see the following pupils in my room *immediately*."

Pencils froze in mid-sentence. Mr Fairbrother's voice was icy and menacing.

"Billy Simpkins, Keith Hall, Christine Robinson and Matthew Evans."

Billy, Keith and Christine stood up at once, but Matthew was still fidgeting with his pencil case, desperately trying to put his felt-tips back.

"*Now*, Matthew!" boomed Mr Fairbrother.

Matthew dropped his pens on the floor in fright.

"Leave them where they are and come with me," commanded Mr Fairbrother. Matthew scuttled to the door, his bottom lip already trembling.

"And as for the rest of you . . . " Mr Fairbrother glared at the class, "I'll be back to deal with you later!"

Mr Fairbrother didn't say another word until the four children were lined up in front of the desk in his room.

"Before we begin I want to make a few things perfectly plain. I am going to ask you some simple, straightforward questions; and I want some plain, straightforward answers. I am very, very cross with the four of you, and I am in *no* mood for any of the usual nonsense. If anybody says 'I dunno, sir' I will probably throttle them. Is everything clear so far?"

Billy, Keith and Christine nodded; Matthew nodded and sniffed.

"*And* I cannot bear children who snivle. Tempting as it is, I am not actually going to murder anybody. You're not infants; you're all in Class Four. People who are going to burst into tears the moment they get into trouble would do better not to get into trouble in the first place. So for heaven's sake, Matthew, blow your nose and pull yourself together."

Matthew hiccuped, sniffed, and wiped his nose on the sleeve of his blazer. Mr Fairbrother closed his eyes until the grisly performance was over.

"Good. If everybody is ready, I'll begin. Half an hour ago I received a phone call from the vicar of All Souls Church. It seems that yester-day afternoon, after school, the four of you were in the graveyard of the church up to no good. Or, to be strictly accurate, Billy, Keith and Christine were actually *in* the grave-yard. Matthew was half-in and half-out of the graveyard, and had to be released by the Fire Brigade. Is that right?"

No one disagreed. Mr Fairbrother continued: "And it also appears that this little performance of yours attracted quite a crowd – approximately twenty or thirty other children. Is everything I've said correct so far?"

All four children nodded.

"Good. And it would seem from Matthew's hysterical screaming that he was under the impression that he was about to be attacked by a ghost. So much so, Matthew, that I understand you actually bit Mr Wilbury, the gardener, on the hand when he tried to free your head from the railings. Is that true?"

"Y-yes, Mr F-F-Fairbrother."

"Well, we seem to be making progress, so far. But now we come to the part you always seem to find so difficult: I want the whole story – beginning, middle and end, and in that order, if at all possible. I want to know every-thing, do you understand – *everything*.

"Billy – I think I'll start with you. Just answer

one question at a time. When exactly did this whole ghost business begin . . . ?"

Mr Fairbrother listened carefully as the whole story unravelled. As usual, it turned out to be quite simple and – in its own peculiar way – perfectly logical. As he listened, Mr Fairbrother found himself marvelling once again at the way children's minds worked: they'd noticed tiny details that no adult would spot in a hundred years, put them all together and . . . come up with completely the wrong answer! Mr Fairbrother couldn't help thinking of Sherlock Holmes. It was as if Holmes's astonishing powers of observation had been coupled with the reasoning powers of the average sheep.

"How on earth can we teach them anything?" he found himself wondering. "They don't think like adults, they don't act like adults – they're a completely different species!"

"So that's the full story, is it?"

The children nodded.

"Well, all that remains now," said Mr Fairbrother, "is to decide what I'm going to do with you."

He paused, and looked at the four worried faces.

"You've caused a lot of trouble, especially to poor Mr Wilbury. I'll be writing to your parents today" – all four children looked suddenly

75

horrified – "to tell them what you've been up to. And I'm also going to suggest to them that you should spend at least two days of your summer holidays helping Mr Wilbury to weed the graveyard – I think it's the very least you can do to make amends.

"And I've asked Mr Wilbury to come into school this afternoon. I want you – and the rest of Class Four, I haven't forgotten that the rest of them were involved – to apologise to him in person. Any questions?

"Now, I think we've wasted quite enough time on this nonsense. Go back to your classroom, get on with your work, and don't let me ever hear of you four going ghost-hunting again."

The children filed out.

Mr Fairbrother sighed. That was the one part of the job he really disliked: playing the heavy. He looked at his watch; another morning nearly over, and still the pile of paperwork was untouched.

The phone rang.

Wearily Mr Fairbrother picked up the receiver: "Hello?"

"Hello," replied a business-like voice at the other end. "This is the County Finance Department. It's about your school dinner-money for last week. Could I please speak to Mr Fairbrother?"

Mr Fairbrother closed his eyes, and crossed his fingers.

"I'm terribly sorry," he said politely, "but I think you must have the wrong number."

And he replaced the receiver.

Eleven

As Class Four filed into the classroom after lunch, there was none of the usual chattering and jostling. The children were subdued and quiet. They all knew who was coming to visit them that afternoon, and they were worried.

A visitor in the classroom usually meant that something exciting was going to happen, but Mr Wilbury wasn't that kind of visitor. Would he be cross with them? Would he shout at them? Would he be allowed to punish them in some way? Nobody knew.

Mr Parker opened his drawer, took out the register and his special register pen, and called out the children's names in an eery silence. As he called the last name, "Billy Simpkins?", there was a knock at the door.

All the children immediately stiffened and sat up very straight, arms folded.

"Come in!" called Mr Parker – and in walked Melanie Davies from Class Two.

"Please, Mr Parker, Mrs Gurdon says, can she borrow your staple gun?"

Melanie looked nervously around her. She often ran errands for Mrs Gurdon, but she'd never had a class snap to attention when she walked into a room before.

"Yes, of course, Melanie."

Mr Parker opened his drawer. Class Four let out a huge sigh of relief.

"Here you are, dear."

Mr Parker handed the staple gun to Melanie with a smile.

Melanie took the staple gun, but didn't smile back.

"T-thank you, Mr P-Parker," she stammered, and sidled nervously out of the room. She hadn't realised Mr Parker was so strict. All the children in Class Four were obviously terrified of him!

She fled back to the cosy chaos of Mrs Gurdon's room.

Back in Class Four, Mr Parker was taking full advantage of the situation.

"We'll have silent reading," he announced, certain for once that it would be silent. "And if you've finished your reading books, you can go to the school library to change it – but no more than two people at a time."

Christine and Deirdre put their hands up first and left the room, clutching their books. Billy and Keith were next, and waited patiently for the two girls to return.

The eery stillness continued.

Billy slumped forward on his desk, his head in his hands.

Keith nudged him on the arm.

"Billy?" he whispered.

But Billy shook his head without even looking up.

Keith was bored. He turned his book over and started to read the blurb on the back cover.

WELLY! The hilarious adventures of a boy who wakes up one morning to discover that he has turned into a giant gumboot.

Keith opened the book, and read the dedication: "To Harvey Mendham, my wonderful English teacher," it said. "With love and gratitude."

"What a creep!" thought Keith. He couldn't imagine that any English teacher would be at all flattered by having a useless book like *Welly!* dedicated to him.

Christine and Deirdre returned.

"Billy and Keith," called out Mr Parker, "you can go and change your books now."

After the sombre quiet of the classroom, it was a relief for Billy and Keith to be out in the corridor. They walked along, enjoying the normal hub-bub of conversation that spilled out of the other classrooms.

But as they turned the corner, and began to walk past the cloakrooms, they saw a tall figure dressed in shabby brown moleskins and an old-fashioned collarless shirt coming out of Mr Fairbrother's room at the far end of the corridor. It was Mr Wilbury!

The two boys darted round the corner and sprinted back to their classroom. They burst through the door, white-faced and breathless.

Mr Parker jumped with surprise.

"Billy! Keith! Don't you know better than to come hurtling into a room like that? And what on earth's the matter? You look as if you've just seen a gh—" He just managed to stop himself saying it in time.

"It's him!" gasped Billy. "Mr Wilbury! And he's coming down the corridor *now*!"

"Well, in that case, you'd better calm down, and go and sit in your place," said Mr Parker. He turned to face the rest of the class: "Mr Wilbury will be with us shortly, so put your books away and sit quietly until he arrives."

There was a frantic scurrying as children rushed to put their books away in their trays. As the last child sat down, there was a knock on the door.

"Come in!" called Mr Parker.

The door opened, and in came Mr Fairbrother and Mr Wilbury.

Mr Wilbury and Mr Parker shook hands. As they did, the children could clearly see a new sticking plaster on Mr Wilbury's right hand.

"This is Mr Wilbury," announced Mr Fairbrother. "Mr Wilbury works at All Souls Church. You all know why he's here this afternoon. I believe you have something to say to him. Billy?"

Billy got to his feet. Although he'd been going over and over his speech in his head, his legs felt like jelly and his hands were sweaty and trembling. He took a deep breath: "We would all like to say that we're very sorry for all the trouble we caused . . . um, especially me and Keith and Christine and Matthew . . . and . . . er . . . and we promise we won't do it again."

Billy stared down at his feet, thoroughly embarrassed.

"Thank you, Billy," said Mr Fairbrother. "You may sit down. And now, I think Mr Wilbury would like to say a few words to you. Mr Wilbury?"

"What I've got to say is this," began Mr Wilbury, awkwardly. "There are some places which are places to play, and some places which aren't. And graveyards . . . well, graveyards and churches are supposed to be peaceful places; places where people like to go to think and be quiet. What I'm trying to say is, next time you want to let off a bit of steam, go to the park or somewhere. Okay? And as for all this ghost business . . . well . . . "

He stopped, and scratched his head.

"Look," he said, "I'm not much good at making speeches – as you can probably tell." He looked across at Mr Parker and Mr Fairbrother. "Do you mind if I sit down?" he asked.

"Of course not," replied Mr Fairbrother, pointing to the teacher's chair at the front.

Mr Wilbury turned the chair round to face the class and sat down.

He looked over his shoulder to Mr Fairbrother and Mr Parker. "If you two gentlemen don't mind, I reckon that what I'm trying to say would be better said in a story . . . would that be all right? It shouldn't take more than, well, ten minutes or so?"

Mr Fairbrother looked at Mr Parker, then back at Mr Wilbury.

"It's Mr Parker's class," he replied, "but if he doesn't mind, then I've got no objections. Mr Parker?"

"Well . . . I . . . I . . . " Mr Parker was taken aback. He didn't want to sound rude or ungrateful to a guest. He pulled himself together. "If it's no trouble, Mr Wilbury. If you've got better things to do – that is, don't feel you have to. After all, it's the children who have to apologise to you. They're the ones who are in the wrong."

Mr Parker didn't mean to sound ungracious, but he didn't like surprises; he didn't like his classroom routine disrupted.

"As I said, it shouldn't take long," Mr Wilbury assured him. He turned to face the class. "It's about something that happened to me, when I was about your age, maybe a little older. I had a similar experience: I thought I saw a ghost. And, like you lot, I made a bit of a fool of myself, too."

Twelve

"It all happened more than fifty years ago," said Mr Wilbury, "when I was eleven years old and I had to leave the school I'd been going to since I was five and start at the big secondary. I expect that'll happen to you, too.

I knew a bit about my new school because my big brother, Alf, had been there for two years. And on the first day we both got on the bus together. But Alf wouldn't sit with me; I was only a first year and he was a third year. He went and sat with his mates – Wilkie and Thompson – and I was left on my own, at the back of the bus, while they all laughed and joked, and showed off to the girls on the bus.

Everything about my new school was big – the buildings, the playground, the sports fields. But the biggest, and most frightening thing in the whole school was Mr Wainwright, the headmaster. He was a great ox of a man. He was the biggest man that most of us had seen in our entire lives. He must have been six foot four or five, and he had hands like bundles of pork chops.

On the first morning, all the first years had

85

to stay behind after assembly. Mr Wainwright gave us a long talk on the school rules – what we were allowed to do, and what we weren't allowed to do. Most of it was what we weren't allowed to do. No running in the corridors, no sweets in school, no talking in the dinner queues . . . the list went on and on. The last item on the *Don't List* was The Grange.

When he got to this part Old Wainwright seemed to swell to twice his usual size, and his great booming voice filled the enormous hall.

'Boys and girls,' he said, in a voice like thunder, 'on your way into school this morning you may have noticed the old house opposite the school, The Grange. It has been empty for many years, and is now extremely unsafe. Last year a number of pupils thought it clever to play in that house. It is not clever, or brave, boys and girls. It is extremely stupid. The Grange is strictly out of bounds. Any boy or girl found playing there will be dealt with *most severely*. Is that clear?'

Nobody said a word. It wasn't the kind of question you were supposed to answer.

Three days later we found out what he meant by *most severely*.

On that day, we came in from lunch and the register was taken, as usual. But instead of starting work as normal, we were lined up and marched into the hall. We were going to have a 'special assembly', our teacher said.

We all filed into the hall in silence. Nobody knew what was happening.

Standing on the stage was Mr Wainwright, the headmaster. He was wearing a long black gown, and he had his hands behind his back. Three boys were also on the stage – Wilkie and Thompson, my brother's mates, and a third boy called Martins. And in the centre of the stage, between Mr Wainwright and the three boys, was one of the long, low benches we used for PE.

When everyone was sitting down, still and quiet, Old Wainwright brought his right hand out from behind his back with a flourish. Gripped in his huge paw was a cane.

'Boys and girls!' he thundered. 'Despite my warnings, and the severe punishments I gave last year, children still persist in playing in The Grange. This disobedience will stop – *now*! These boys' – and he pointed with the cane at Wilkie, Thompson and Martins – 'were caught returning from The Grange during a *mathematics lesson!* I have been too lenient for too long. Starting today, any boy *or* girl found playing near The Grange will be caned in front of the whole school! Do I make myself plain?'

No one said a word.

Wainwright flexed the cane in his huge hands.

'Wilkie!' he boomed. 'Step forward.'

One by one, the three boys walked forward, bent over the bench, and got three of the best. Then each had to shake Mr Wainwright by the hand and go back to his place on the stage.

When the whole performance was over Old Wainwright glared at the rest of us from the stage.

'Let that be a lesson to all of you!' he bellowed. 'School – *dis*-missed!'

On the bus going home I was allowed to sit with Alf and his pals. What an honour to be allowed to sit with the Great Wilkie! Except that I wasn't actually sitting *with* Wilkie, because Wilkie stood up all the way.

When we got home, I asked Alf what sort of games they played over at The Grange. Alf laughed.

'They weren't playing any stupid kids' games over there,' he said. 'They were over there on a dare. They were down by the pond.'

'What's so daring about that?' I asked.

'Don't you know about The Grange?' Alf asked. 'Haven't you heard about what happened there?'

And what Alf told me went like this. The Grange had been built about fifty years before

by a very rich man – a millionaire, in fact – who'd made his fortune mining for gold and diamonds in Africa. He'd decided to come home to England, and get a place in the country where he could relax and enjoy himself. Like a lot of rich men he had a lot of friends, and the thing he loved best was to hold huge parties for them all.

When he came to have The Grange built, he drew all his own plans so that the house would be exactly as he wanted it – a sort of grown-up's playground.

When it was finished, it was huge! There were twenty or thirty bedrooms, a ballroom for dancing, a library, a billiard room; and in the grounds he had tennis courts, two croquet lawns, and a Japanese Water Garden which had a little summer house and a little wooden bridge going over a stream – all copied from the 'Willow Pattern' plates. But his pride and joy was the private boating lake he'd had made at the bottom of the grounds.

It wasn't a real lake, more like a large oval pond, and at one end was a little boat-house where he kept four or five little rowing boats. On fine summer days his guests would row back and forth across the boating lake.

Anyway, one weekend in the middle of summer, the man who owned The Grange was having one of his parties. One of his guests was a young chap who had been making a real pig of himself – the way some people do at parties and Christmas time. He'd had double helpings at dinner the night before, an enormous breakfast, and by the time he was half-way through his lunch he began to feel really bloated and uncomfortable."

Mr Wilbury stopped, and looked at the silent children.

"Did anyone here make a real pig of themselves last Christmas?"

A sprinkling of hands went up.

"Well then, you can probably guess how he felt. Before the meal was over, he excused himself from the table and went outside for a breath of fresh air. He walked through the grounds – round the tennis courts, past the croquet lawns, through the Japanese Water Garden – and down to the boating lake.

When he got to the lake he stood there for a while just looking at the water. Then he got an idea. 'That's what I need,' he thought, 'a cool refreshing swim.'

So he looked all round to make sure no one was watching, then he took off all his clothes and dived in.

Now I'm sure that your mums or dads or teachers have told you – never go swimming just after you've eaten. Unfortunately, nobody had ever told this young chap and just as he reached the middle of the pond he got the most dreadful cramp. His arm and leg muscles locked, and he couldn't swim any more.

Desperately, he started thrashing around in the water and screaming for help as loudly as he could, but he was getting weaker and weaker and swallowing more and more water. Then just as he was giving up hope two men came running to opposite sides of the pond, and dived in to try and save him: the man who owned The Grange, and one of his guests.

The guest swam to the middle, grabbed the young chap as he was going down for the third time, and managed to drag him to the bank – where he was *very* sick, but otherwise all right.

But after a minute or two, they both realised something was terribly wrong – the man who owned The Grange wasn't anywhere to be seen.

Later that afternoon the police arrived and started dragging the pond. They took out two of the rowing boats from the little boat-house, tied chains to the back with big grappling-hooks on the end, and rowed back and forth across the pond. They dragged the pond until nightfall, but they found nothing.

Next day, they came back and tried again. But once more, although they dragged the pond until dark, they never found his body. He'd dived into the pond, and simply disappeared – and no trace of him was ever found!"

Thirteen

"That was the story Alf told me. Two days later I was standing in the playground, minding my own business, when Wilkie came up to me. He had a mean look on his face.

'Where's Alf?' he said. 'He's not in class today.'

'In bed,' I said. 'He's got the flu.'

'Well, he owes me two bob' – that's ten pence, in modern money – 'and I need it, *now*. You're his brother, so you give it to me.'

I hadn't got two bob. But even if I had, I wouldn't have given it to him. Although I was only a first year I was big for my age, and I *wasn't* going to be bossed around – even by Wilkie.

'Nothing to do with me,' I said, trying to look as big and mean as Wilkie.

'I want my money back, and I'm going to get it,' he said, bunching up his fists.

'Oh, yeah?' I said. 'And how are you going to do that?'

He hit me!

So I hit him back – harder.

Then he grabbed me round the neck, and

94

I grabbed him round the waist. Suddenly we were on the ground, punching and wrestling.

'Fight!' yelled someone, and almost immediately we were surrounded by a shrieking circle of boys – and a few girls – all yelling us on as we punched and gouged and clawed at each other.

It ended with both of us getting the cane from Old Wainwright – three of the best and, blimey, it hurt like nothing I'd ever felt before.

During dinner break, Wilkie came up to me again.

'You're a dirty little fighter, aren't you?' he said.

I didn't say anything, just got my fists ready for what I was sure would happen next.

But it didn't.

'Do you want to be in my gang?' asked Wilkie.

Of course I did. What an honour! No first year had ever been allowed to join a third-year gang before.

'Yeah!' I said, really proud.

'Right, you're in . . . as long as you can pass the test.'

'What's the test?' I asked.

'You've got to go into The Grange and get a jam-jar of water from the old pond,' he replied. 'Tomorrow.'

That night I hardly slept a wink. I kept thinking about the body in the pond, and Wainwright and his cane. Every time I dropped off to sleep, the two merged into one horrible nightmare of Wainwright rising out of the pond, cane in hand, coming to get me!

The next day was a Friday. When school finished for the day, me and Wilkie and the rest of the gang walked out of the gate as normal and started to walk down the hill towards the bus stop. But as soon as we were out of sight of the school, we ducked through a gap in the hedge that surrounded the school field, and lay in the ditch waiting for the coast to clear.

One by one, the teachers pushed their bicycles on to the road and pedalled off down the hill. We watched them through the gap in the hedge, mentally ticking them off as they cycled past us: Mr Wharton – first as always. Miss Cherry, followed very closely by Mr Nugent (we all knew about Miss Cherry and Mr Nugent!). Mr Wheeler, scruffy as a scarecrow on his rusty old bone-shaker, nearly falling off because he got the bottom of his frayed trousers caught in the chain. Then finally – off to tend his rose garden – Mr Wainwright, back as straight as a ram-rod, like a cavalry officer on his enormous green Raleigh.

The coast was clear. We scrambled back

through the gap in the hedge, and crossed the road to the tall iron gates at the bottom of the drive that led to The Grange.

Wilkie handed me the jam-jar.

'I'll keep watch,' he said.

I squeezed through a gap in the fence, beside the locked gates, and started to walk slowly up the drive.

The grounds were nothing like what I'd imagined in my dreams of the night before. I'd been expecting a sort of overgrown garden – weedy and messy, but still recognisably a garden – but this was a jungle! I could see nothing either side of the gravel drive but a dense wall of half-wild rhododendrons and laurel trees.

I stopped at the first bend in the drive and looked back. But I couldn't even see the gates for the dense mass of overgrown shrubs. It was as if the shrubs, having parted to let me in, had closed in behind me – cutting off my way out, trapping me in the haunted grounds!

Slowly I crept on, up the drive towards the house.

The house itself was an empty shell, a skeleton of crumbling brick and jutting timbers. Black shadows seemed to move and swirl behind the smashed windows. The door was open – hanging from broken hinges – and I was sure that I could hear the scrit-scrat of rats scurrying away as I crept closer.

To the left of the house stood a long dark passageway of entwined branches – an old yew walk. That was my route. I began to tiptoe down the dank, foul-smelling tunnel – slowly at first, then faster and faster until I was sprinting towards the growing circle of daylight at the end. I burst into the light and stood panting for breath.

In front of me was a wide meadow of waist-high grass. I wondered, at first, if I'd somehow come the wrong way and blundered on to a neighbouring farm. Slowly I realised that this must be all that was left of the lawns that Alf had told me about. It had to be, for there, in the distance, I could see the denser green of reeds that marked the edge of the old pond.

I waded through the grass, leaving a flattened wake behind me. I could see other faint trails leading in the same direction.

As the slight slope of the meadow became steeper, I noticed that the grass had changed, become coarser. Green spears of reeds began jutting up, and my feet began to squelch in the marshier ground. Suddenly I found myself struggling through reeds. Water lapped over my shoes. I looked around me: I was at the edge of the stagnant pond.

With a mixture of relief and dread, I stooped down and plunged my jam-jar into the brown water and scooped it out again. Only half-full. I pushed it down into the water again . . .

But as I did, I became aware of a slight movement in the water, beyond the reeds. I looked up. Bubbles were breaking the surface about ten metres from where I squatted.

As slowly as in a nightmare, I got to my feet. The bubbles were closer; and I could tell they were too big for a frog, too big for a fish. I could see a monstrous shape – a blur of green and yellow – gliding through the water towards me.

I dropped the jar and ran for my life. Across the meadow I sprinted, down the yew walk, and burst into the drive. I tore down it, yelling my head off as if all the fiends of hell were after me!

I shot through the gap in the fence and out on to the road. Wilkie and the others had heard me, and they were already running down the hill. I sprinted after them, yelling for them to wait for me.

And we never, ever, went near that old house again!"

Fourteen

The story was over. The children let out their breath in one huge sigh.

"How many of you think I saw a ghost?" asked Mr Wilbury.

Every hand went up.

Mr Wilbury laughed. "Now I'm going to do something no good story-teller would ever do – I'm going to tell you what happened next. And I'm afraid you're in for a disappointment.

A couple of years later The Grange was sold. The people who bought it wanted to build houses on the land, so the first thing they did was to pull down the old house. Next, they had to level the site – and that meant draining the old pond for starters.

By that time my brother Alf had left school and was waiting to go into the army. He got a job as a casual labourer, clearing the land around The Grange. His first job on the site was to help drain the old pond!

He was worried sick, as you can imagine. So was I. And we were sitting in the kitchen, the night before he was due to start, wondering what to do, when my dad came in.

101

He took one look at us and said, 'What's up, boys? You two look proper poorly.'

So we told him all about Alf having to drain the pond, and all about the bloke who'd drowned. I told him what I'd seen that Friday evening, too.

And he just sat in his chair and roared with laughter.

'What a couple of winnets!' he said, and laughed even more.

When he got his breath back, and wiped his eyes, he told us the true story.

It was true that, many years before, in a big house nearby, a man had died trying to save someone who'd got into difficulties while swimming. In fact, he hadn't drowned but died of a heart attack. And it wasn't a young man he'd saved but a young woman. And he hadn't made a fortune out of gold and diamonds, but from writing musical plays for the theatre.

But the biggest difference between the two stories was the house. The swimming accident hadn't happened at The Grange at all, but in another house about two miles away. The man who'd built The Grange had made a fortune, but he went bankrupt just as he was about to move in. The Grange had never actually been lived in. It was what it had always been – derelict.

So I couldn't have seen a ghost, could I?"

Mr Wilbury looked around him at the disappointed faces. He grinned.

"But I did see *something* – I hadn't gone completely barmy.

Alf came back the next day and told us that when they drained the pond they *had* found something. In amongst all the weeds and mud in the bottom, they found the body of a huge pike. How it got there, nobody could work out. But there it was, and it must have been that huge fish I saw that afternoon."

Mr Fairbrother and Mr Parker stood at the staffroom window watching Mr Wilbury – surrounded by an eager crowd of excited children – making his way slowly across the playground to the gates.

"Living history," said Mr Fairbrother, sipping his coffee. "I wish I'd thought to switch on a tape-recorder. Let's hope it's put an end to the ghost-hunting craze, and all the other nonsense we've been having from Class Four lately. I don't know what gets into them sometimes, I really don't. Did you know, Mr Parker, there was some kind of rumour going around that there was a dragon living in the sand-pit? I picked that up on the Infant grapevine, but apparently it all started with some daft game your lot were playing. Terrified the life out of

Miss Moneypenny's class – you can't get them to do a standing broad jump for love or money! Puzzling where they pick these ideas up from, isn't it? What's the matter, Mr Parker? You're choking – is the coffee too hot?"

Mr Parker got his breath back, but he was still rather red in the face.

"Well . . . er, actually I think it might have been . . . me!" he admitted.

"You, Mr Parker? And why should you wish to terrorise the reception class with tales of dragons?"

"No, what I meant was – it was me that told Class Four. We've been doing a project on King Arthur and the Knights of the Round Table. I'm sorry if it's caused any problems, Mr Fairbrother . . . it seemed a good idea at the time."

But Mr Fairbrother had stopped listening to Mr Parker, and was staring out of the window. He was watching Billy Simpkins and Keith Hall. Instead of walking out of the school gates with Mr Wilbury and all the other children, Billy and Keith were running back across the playground in the direction of the kitchens. As Mr Fairbrother watched, the two boys disappeared behind the dustbins. They re-emerged a couple of seconds later waving two sticks.

From the way he was flourishing it, it was

clear to Mr Fairbrother that Billy's stick was supposed to be some kind of sword; Keith's stick was shorter, and from the way he was stabbing and jabbing with it, Mr Fairbrother guessed it was supposed to be a dagger or knife.

The two boys ran across the playground and out of the school gates, brandishing their weapons.

"Ah-ha!" exclaimed Mr Fairbrother. "Things are beginning to fall into place . . . "

Mr Parker broke into his train of thought. "Do you think I should, well, try and repair the damage in some way? Maybe I could apologise to Miss Moneypenny. What do you think, Mr Fairbrother?"

Mr Fairbrother turned round from the window. He smiled at Mr Parker. "Yes," he said. "Yes, I think there is something you could do to make amends." He paused. "Tell me, Mr Parker, are you any good at adding up dinner-money?"

Other great reads *from* **Red Fox**

Other great reads ⌇*from* **Red Fox**

THE SNIFF STORIES   Ian Whybrow

Things just keep happening to Ben Moore. It's dead hard
avoiding disaster when you've got to keep your street cred with
your mates *and* cope with a family of oddballs at the same time.
There's his appalling 2½ year old sister, his scatty parents who
are into healthy eating and animal rights and, worse than all
of these, there's Sniff! If only Ben could just get on with his
scientific experiments and his attempt at a world beating
Swampbeast score . . . but there's no chance of that while chaos
is just around the corner.

ISBN 0 09 975040 6   £2.99

J.B. SUPERSLEUTH   Joan Davenport

James Bond is a small thirteen-year-old with spots and
spectacles. But with a name like that, how can he help being
a supersleuth?

It all started when James and 'Polly' (Paul) Perkins spotted
a teacher's stolen car. After that, more and more mysteries
needed solving. With the case of the Arabian prince, the
Murdered Model, the Bonfire Night Murder and the Lost
Umbrella, JB's reputation at Moorside Comprehensive soars.

But some of the cases aren't quite what they seem . . .

ISBN 0 09 971780 8   £2.99